Text copyright © 2009 by Kate Banks

Pictures copyright © 2009 by Georg Hallensleben

Distributed in Canada by Douglas & McIntyre Ltd.

Printed in February 2009 in China by South China Printing Co. Ltd.,

Dongguan City, Guangdong Province

Designed by Jaclyn Sinquett

1   3   5   7   9   10   8   6   4   2

www.fsgkidsbooks.com

Library of Congress Cataloging-in-Publication Data

Banks, Kate, date.

What's coming for Christmas? / Kate Banks ; pictures by Georg Hallensleben.— 1st ed.

p.   cm.

Summary: While a farm family bustles about, preparing for the arrival of Christmas, they do not notice the great anticipation spreading among the animals, who know that something very special is on its way.

ISBN-13: 978-0-374-39948-1

ISBN-10: 0-374-39948-4

[1. Farm animals—Fiction.   2. Birth—Fiction.   3. Christmas—Fiction.]   I. Hallensleben, Georg, ill.   II. Title.

PZ7.B22594 Whd 2009

[E]—dc22

2008020753

Kate Banks   pictures by Georg Hallensleben

What's Coming for Christmas?

FRANCES FOSTER BOOKS
Farrar, Straus and Giroux
New York

Something was coming.
You could see it in the way the snow whirled and twirled,
making hills and bumps.
In the way the children lay in snowbanks making angels,
their arms spread wide as if to say, "Welcome."

Something was coming.
You could see it in the way the snowman's eyes sparkled.
And in the way icicles dripped in the sun like hourglasses
counting the seconds.

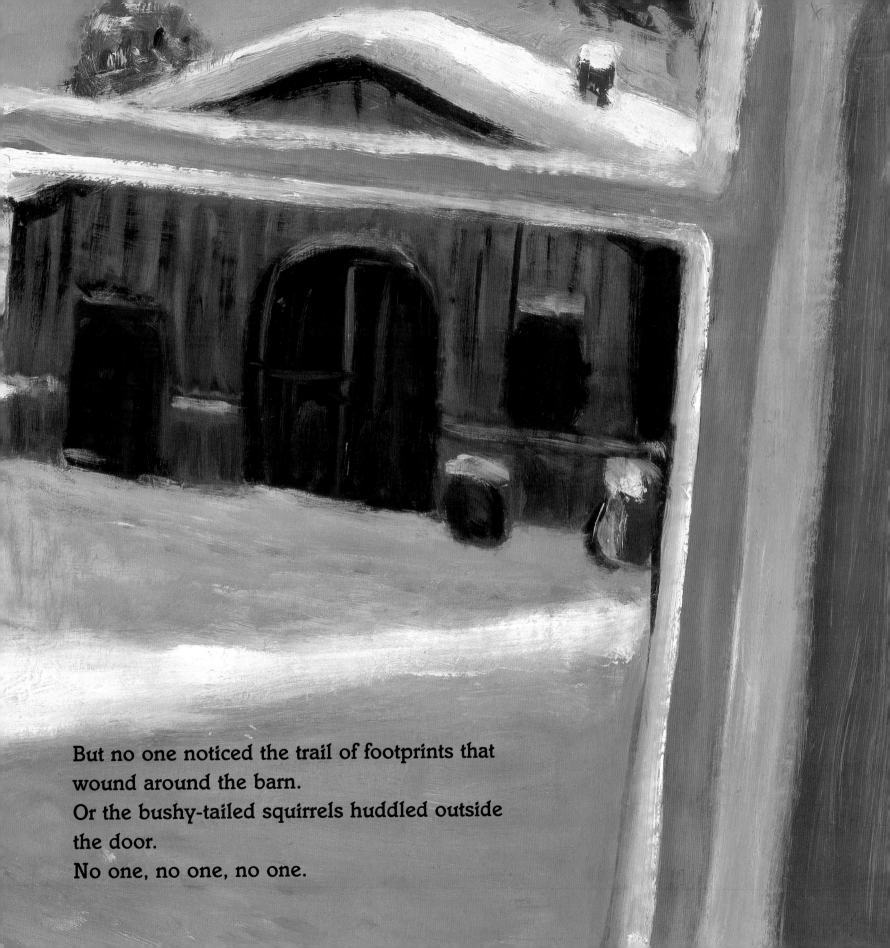

But no one noticed the trail of footprints that
wound around the barn.
Or the bushy-tailed squirrels huddled outside
the door.
No one, no one, no one.

Something was coming.
You could hear it in the voices of carolers that
echoed through the streets.
And in the chime of church bells.

You could hear it in the crinkle of wrapping paper and the hiss of scissors curling ribbon.
In the flutter of paper snowflakes pressed against the windowpanes.
In the happy cries of children trimming the tree.

But no one heard the jingle of cowbells.
Or the shushing of the mother hen quieting
her chicks.
No one, no one, no one.

Something was coming.
You could smell it in the scent of cinnamon
and spice that permeated the air.
In the odor of pine that tickled your nose each
time you passed through the hallway.

You could feel it in the stiff winter air that
hovered around doors and window frames,
begging to come in.
In the warm fire dancing in the hearth.
In the stockings asking to be filled.
Something was coming.

But no one noticed the pigs' little tails curled
in excitement.
Or the ears of the billy goat upright and alert.
No one, no one, no one.

Something was coming.
You could see it in the way the children crowded
around the manger.
In the way the three wise men solemnly offered gifts.

But no one noticed the barn lights begin to blink.
Or the sheep who nodded knowingly to one another as if to say,
"It won't be long now."
No one, no one, no one.

Something was coming.
You could taste it in the sugarcoated air that wafted through the house.
In the cookies spread across the counter.
In the gingerbread house trimmed with mounds of white icing.

But no one noticed the fresh bed of hay in a corner of the barn.
Or the wide-eyed winter owl who stood watch.
No one, no one, no one.

Something was coming.
You could see it in the way the frost made patterns
on the windowpanes as if writing a secret message.
You could feel it in the way the children tossed fitfully in their sleep.
In the way the mother horse paced back and forth in her stall.
Something was coming.

No one heard the jingle of sleigh bells approaching as the clock
struck midnight.
No one saw who put the gifts under the tree and filled the stockings.
Or who ate the plate of cookies and carrots left on the table.
No one, no one, no one.

No one heard the quickening of life as the new pony entered the world.
Or saw the mouse running to spread the news.
And no one knew who placed the star above the horses' stall.

But in the morning, everyone knew that something had come.